ROCKET RACERS

STEVE WEBB ★ BEN MANTLE

PICTURE CORGI

Space rocket, race racket,
race to the **moon**...

Starship Spike!

Blast off, fast off,
moon race night!

Up and up in outer space,

supernova bright,

rockets racing to the **moon**, a **supersonic** sight.

Zoomers, zappers, outer spacers, rocket racket lunar racers.

Faster! Faster! Rocket blaster!
Racer, chaser, rocket master!

Race track, fast track,

zig, zag, zoom!

Spike and **Space Ball** in a jam,
tangled up in flight.

Could this be
the end of their
space race night?

BOXER ROCKET
zips away,
a race to be won,

but racing all
alone, is **NOT**
as much fun.

Taking out his
hammer, he knows
just what to do . . .

with his un-jammer banger:

TO THE RESCUE!

Fast track,
race track,
BOXER ROCKET
zooms back . . .

Un-jammer hammer banger,
ready,

steady . . .

WHACK!

Rock it, BOXER ROCKET,

WHACK IT!

10

5

Bang it, clang it, what a racket!
Bend it, mend it, bash it back . . .

BOXER ROCKET, Starship Spike and **Space Ball** reach the moon.

They land together, with a clang,
a dusty banger boom!

How can they decide who is the fastest of the three?

Fast track, race track,
everybody race back!
Blast off, fast off,
ready,
steady
ZOOM!

Rocket racers,
outer spacers,
come again soon!

For the completely lovely and rather
noisy Zoe, Daniel and Romey, with love

– Steve Webb

For Andy, Rachael and Lily

– Ben Mantle

ROCKET RACERS
A PICTURE CORGI BOOK 978 0 552 57594 2
Published in Great Britain by Picture Corgi, an imprint of Random House Children's Publishers UK
A Random House Group Company
This edition published 2013
3 5 7 9 10 8 6 4 2
Text copyright © Steve Webb, 2013
Illustrations copyright © Ben Mantle, 2013
RANDOM HOUSE CHILDREN'S PUBLISHERS UK, 61–63 Uxbridge Road, London W5 5SA
www.**randomhousechildrens**.co.uk
www.**randomhouse**.co.uk
Addresses for companies within The Random House Group Limited can be found at:
www.randomhouse.co.uk/offices.htm
THE RANDOM HOUSE GROUP Limited Reg. No. 954009
A CIP catalogue record for this book is available from the British Library.
Printed in China